The Canal Monster of Little Ides

Pattison Telford

Published by Pattison Telford, 2020.

THE CANAL MONSTER OF LITTLE IDES

First edition. January 15, 2020.
Copyright © 2020 Pattison Telford.
Written by Pattison Telford.
Cover design by Darin Morrison-Beer.

Also by Pattison Telford

The Canal Monster of Little Ides

Watch for more at https://pattisontelford.com.

The Canal Monster of Little Ides

My grandmother Angelina Redferne is often incoherent now, so she never gives me a straight answer about whether we saw a canal monster on the day that we discovered Disco together.

Seven years ago, I was ten. Granny's hair was less wispy, with a reminder of the violent scarlet still resisting the grey. She was my second greatest hero, eclipsed only by my older brother, Newton. Even as a ten-year-old, intuition told me she was a little wild, regaling us kids lovingly and in great earnestness about a menagerie of imaginary things. Bedtime stories were better with her than with my mother, who described things like the scientist she was.

That's why I looked forward to that late spring afternoon. My mother had taken my little sister on a museum trip to London, and my father was away on business. I thought he said his visit was to Berzerkistan, but I can see now that he either went to some properly named country that I misheard, or he invented the name to tickle my imagination. Newton had rugby practice that afternoon, so my instructions were to leave right after the final bell from Giant Grove Junior School and meet Granny at our family's narrowboat which lay moored nearby on the Royal Canal.

I like everything orderly. Backpack on, school jacket buttoned from the bottom up, I walked out of the schoolyard, along the street, and over the canal via a humpy walking bridge. It looked more like some scrap metal from a wrecker's yard that had accidentally fallen across the canal than an actual bridge. I made a mental note to update its name to the accidental bridge on my hand-drawn map of the town of Middle Ides.

It took only 1742 steps to get to the bridge's centre, and then I started a new count, seeing as how I was crossing the canal's midpoint. The remainder—689 steps—paced out on the towpath beside the canal. I kept counting even while I waved to Granny Angelina, standing on the narrowboat's roof. She looked like she was beckoning to a rescue team, one hand making sweeping waves overhead while the other shielded her eyes from the slanting afternoon sunshine that glinted off the bright red paintwork of our boat.

"Faraday! You're the first mate! Untie that line and hop on."

If you haven't seen a canal narrowboat before, you can probably guess they are narrow. If you were a good jumper, a determined running leap would clear the canal, and two narrowboats can squeeze past side by side. You might also know that they are between seven and ten times as long as they are wide. But you may not know how solid they are—they have thick metal hulls and roof—or how slow they are. Even at full speed, I can get ahead of the boat if I jump off and run along the towpath. Well, I wouldn't do that, but I have seen Newton do it many times.

I untied the line from the mooring ring and fed it back to my grandmother before she grabbed me by the wrist and hauled me up to the back deck. She used the official mountain climber's grip that I had showed her; it's a much stronger and safer connection when two people grab each other's wrists than if they link hand-in-hand. She walked with an air of practiced balance along the narrow ledge bordering the cabin, sliding her slender left hand along the handrail on the roof-edge as she made her way to the nose.

"Start the engine," she called back over her shoulder as she sprung off the front deck into a two-footed landing on the towpath. She moved like a proper human, not the stiff puppetry of other elderly people I observed. Untying the line at the front end, she pushed us away from the mooring spot. The nose edged out, clearing the boat moored in front, and her jump back would have earned her a swim if it had been any later.

I took a deep breath and savoured the moment of starting the engine. My first ever offer to ignite, but I was keenly ready. I had watched every key turn and every start button push since I could remember. It was exciting, and it was just how I imagined it. The engine took three full seconds to get into rhythm before I released the recessed button. The familiar loud-soft-loud-soft engine purr would be a reassuring background for our little excursion.

Granny returned, striding across the barely arched roof, stepping to the back deck. She flicked down the tiller's long wooden handle and put the narrowboat into forward gear while I stood aloof and rested my chin on the red roof, looking ahead, the prow seeming impossibly far away. With a lurch, we set off. Slowly. Very slowly. Which was good, because it took ages for the heavy boats to change direction, and you don't want a collision in a 20-tonne vehicle. Granny laughed and poked me in the ribs from behind with her sandal-clad foot. "Anchors aweigh!"

It was a Redferne tradition to have a ban on snack consumption before a boat journey was underway. But now that we were properly in the canal's main channel as it headed for the Middle Ides aqueduct, the other Redferne family tradition came into play—vulture-like tearing into any available food. I started speaking as I turned. "Hey Granny, did you bring any..."

The holy grail of snacks materialized in her palm, leading an arm adorned with elaborate copper, leather, and silver bracelets. Sherbet dip dab, with its glorious yellow sachet packaging. This was an area of personal expertise—I knew it brimmed with powder that was 94 percent sugar and 100 percent magic. I may have let out a restrained squeal of pure joy. "You're the best Granny ever!"

Granny smiled and looked ahead to the narrowing marking the aqueduct's first arch to see if there were any challenges or if we could glide along at our current stately pace. I hoovered up the dip dab's powdered joy. The long stretch over the aqueduct was wide enough for only a single narrowboat, with a paved towpath and perilously low railing hugging one side. On the other side, the only barrier between you and a 200-foot tumble into the valley below was fresh air and caution.

Seeing no oncoming traffic across the aqueduct, I had a proposition for her. "May I lean over the edge and look down, if you hold me?"

I implicitly trusted her, but noticed she gave my belt two sharp tugs to make sure it wouldn't snake off, leaving her a handful of trousers without a grandson in them.

I leaned. She gripped. Looking straight down over the aqueduct's edge, the Ides River was a trickle only discernable below as a few glints in the dappled sunlight. My best Titanic impersonation was called for. "I'm on top of the world!"

We proceeded serenely over the arched bridge, waving to our own shadows that appeared on the valley floor far below.

"Did you know, Granny, that I got my first name from someone else's last name?"

She smiled at me, the wrinkles at the outer edges of her eyes accentuated. "Of course I know that. You are named Faraday after the famous scientist Michael Faraday. But you're in good company. Both Newton and your sister Higgs are also lucky enough to be named after famous scientists."

"I guess it's cool," I said. My brother and sister indeed suffered the same naming quirk as I did. "But that means I have two last names and no first name."

She thought about that for a moment. "True. But it's better than having two first names, like the singer Paul Simon or Winnie the Pooh's friend Christopher Robin."

"*Yeah*! Or I could have *one* name, like Beyoncé, or Prince, that dad listens to."

"And did you know that your father has two last names too? I never got married, but your dad's father, his last name was Templeton. So that's why I named your father Templeton Redferne."

"Wait. Templeton is a *last* name? But it sounds like a first name," I said.

"Yes, but that's only because you are accustomed to it as a first name. To me, Newton, Higgs, and Faraday don't seem like other people's last names anymore. They seem like grandchildren names."

Our crossing was almost complete, and we approached the widening between the aqueduct and the Little Ides tunnel. Navigating beside me, Granny tensed up. She checked over her shoulder, peered down at the dark canal surface, and glanced behind again.

"Did you see…" she began, but then decided not to continue. I looked around but saw nothing unusual.

Canal etiquette demands that you pause at the start of a tunnel, turn on the lamp at the prow, and ensure there is no traffic coming the other way before proceeding. I scampered through the cabin, emerged on the front deck, and had a look down the tunnel as my grandmother slowed us to a crawl. It was dark beyond the entrance arch, but I saw a semicircle of sunlight at the other end, so I knew there was no oncoming boat. I shouted across the low narrowboat roof. "It's all clear!"

Putt-putting your way through to the Little Ides tunnel exit is a journey of several minutes. There was no towpath through—the stone walls and arched tunnel ceiling tunnel were all within touching distance as you passed through. The surface was rough, with semi-circular channels where the dynamiters had slid their charges all those years ago. I daydreamed about them blasting out the passage.

The hush and rhythms of the tunnel were the voyage's most mesmerizing parts, and I lay on the narrowboat roof while Granny operated the tiller. The tunnel was dark, but not pitch black—there was the starting end's receding light and the advancing glow of the destination combined with the dimmer boat lights. The rhythmic pulsing of the engine and the occasional clink and course correction as the hull's mass glanced lightly off the canal's sides.

I lay on the roof section nearest the back, so Granny didn't even have to raise her voice to chat to me in my semi-trance state. She asked me a question I hadn't considered previously.

"You know when horses used to pull boats like this, before they had engines—what do you think they did when they came to the tunnel, with no path for the horse to use?"

I remained quiet, enjoying the calmness as we slid elegantly along and waited for her to continue. "Someone had to lie on the boat, stretch out their legs, and push off the walls or the ceiling to move it along. Boys, some younger than you, would hang around the tunnel ends, either to do the 'legging' or to lead horses over the hilltop, meeting the boat at the tunnel exit. The boatmen would give them a little money for the help." I lifted my legs overhead, imagining I had to propel the boat by walking along the ceiling.

The narrowboat bobbed on a pair of waves. That was confusing—there aren't any waves in a canal—it's not an ocean!

Granny looked ahead to the archway dividing the gloom from the sunniness of Little Ides, growing nearer, then had a long look backwards. She turned the engine speed up to maximum, which was still slow, but the boat lurched forward with the extra impulse. "What was that? Did we hit something?"

"No, no, it's nothing, Faraday. Come on down here. You can sit inside in the cabin for a minute."

I clambered down from the roof, finding a perch behind the sturdy door separating the driver's position from the cramped dining area. Granny slid the orchestra of bracelets up on one arm then the other, as if preparing to plunge them into something noxious. She looked ahead and back the way we came as we neared the tunnel end.

I heard a splash behind us, like the near-simultaneous slapping of two giant fish on the water's surface after an exuberant leap. We both peered back, but I spied nothing unusual. "Can I go up front and watch from there as we leave the tunnel, Granny?"

She was still looking backwards, answering absently. "Yes, yes. Go ahead."

The narrowboat's front end edged up to the arch, so I raced through the cabin and erupted onto the deck, bounding to the front. I knelt on the bench and stretched my hands over the prow so they would beat the boat into the sunlight of Little Ides. I smiled at a puppy cavorting on the grassy verge, jogging towards me with no sign of an owner. It was a whippet, with its tongue lolling out one side of its mouth.

The boat was half lit by sunshine and half darkened in the tunnel when it happened.

My grandmother had an edge in her voice as she called out just my name. "Faraday!" It wasn't exactly yelled, but the tone sounded strained and urgent.

Turning to look at her, I felt the narrowboat nose downwards, a little water seeping over the dips in the frame that allowed you to step out to the canal side. She was staring away from me, into the tunnel behind her. But it wasn't that sight that paralyzed me in fright, it was amidships where the horror developed.

Something rope-like—but with the thickness of a telephone pole—was constricting itself around the boat's centre portion. The coil emerged from the inky water, looped across the roof, and disappeared into the waters on the other side. It looked like a rope, but it was clearly *alive.*

Splashing in the canal ahead triggered me to whip around and look. For sure, there would be the head of a sea serpent rising out to devour me. I was wrong, but close. It was the gnarled and slimy tail of a giant snake that I saw emerging from the canal, almost touchable if I dared reach forward. It arched back on itself like a whip preparing to lash. The monster was going in the opposite direction to the narrowboat, with its tail in front of me, it's appalling girth constricting amidships, and the rest of its mystery concealed beneath the murky canal waters.

The escalating barking as the puppy ran with excitement along the canal side merged with my cry of "Granny!" But she was sixty feet from me. I was rooted to the bench, a whirlwind of panic and nausea ripping my decision-making powers away. Jumping off the boat, diving into the cabin, or even cowering in place all seemed like decisions I was powerless to make as the rising tail's shadow descended onto me and droplets of cold water chilled my face. I found I couldn't feel my fingers, but my heart was attempting to break free of my chest. I smelled burning.

Maybe I can't remember the next events clearly because they mostly don't make sense. I don't think my grandmother answered my plea, but I know she would never ignore me if I was in danger. I peeled my eyes away from the foul and scaly tail. What was happening back there? The tunnel's darkness shrouded that half of the boat, but I saw Granny standing tall on the back bench, facing away from me.

And she was singing.

It was not a normal song. It was low and only changing pitch slowly, and it sounded like there were two people singing, slightly out of tune with each other. She had one of her larger silver bracelets held aloft in each hand, as if she was tensing for an Olympic routine.

And then I watched, transfixed—all the barking and the threat of a monstrous tail fading into the background. For beyond my grandmother, two glowing yellow eyes that looked like they were lit from behind by flickering flames faced her from the deeper dark beyond. And then two more eyes joined it.

The outline of two bloated serpentine heads emerged from the darkness as the narrowboat continued its slow, relentless drift. A forked black tongue flicked rapidly in and out of each toothy, tiny-nostril'd snout. The steel hull creaked, and the roof bent a little under the monster's coiling ensnarement.

Maybe it was simply the boat's rear nearing the sunlight of Little Ides, but the two bracelets my chanting grandmother held above her took on a brilliant orange glow. The arched ceiling above her burned orange. How did she think some glowing bracelets would protect her from the two grotesque snake heads of the canal monster? I flinched and half-turned away, unable to watch but also scared to look away as one set of jaws opened and darted right at my grandmother. I screamed, but it would not escape my throat.

The threatened venomous fangs' strike never arrived. Instead the head recoiled, like a hand jerking away from a hot stove element. At the same time, I was splattered with spray from a thrashing in the water behind my cowering, hunched back.

I swivelled again, certain I would have one last shocking revelation before I died. But the serpent's tail retreated, waving and slithering down toward the canal's surface, forming an 'S' shape as it retreated. And lodged right near the tail's tip tail was a growling whippet puppy, jaws straining wide as it gripped monster flesh, joining its path through the air then dipping into the canal water.

The singing at the rear had descended into a low growl now. I tried to look both directions—for Granny and to the ripples where the puppy had gone under. In my peripheral vision, she flung the pair of illuminated bracelets toward the canal monster's twin heads. They seemed to expand as they flew, with each one encircling a nightmarish skull like a thrown horseshoe spiralling around a stake. The singing stopped. The bracelets dimmed, sliding in unison down the scale-encrusted necks and the two heads slapped backwards in unison into the tunnel water like a knocked-out boxer toppling onto the canvas.

The tail rippled in an underwater rush back toward me, then disappeared under the boat. I last saw its tapered end as it spiralled around the narrowboat's centre—the hideous coil released its hold like the spring-loaded power cord of a vacuum cleaner recoiling crazily. A drenched puppy head bobbed to the surface so close to me that I felt a little spray as it emerged. The puppy cried out with an excited yipping.

I encouraged my new whippet hero to paddle over to me, and I leaned down and scooped her to safety. One ear was bloodied and incised from her combat, but she didn't seem to notice. She shook and then jumped all over me, licking and barking excitedly.

Granny was calling out in a panic, "Faraday! Faraday, where are you?"

I popped my head above the roof so she could see my face, and shouted, "I'm okay Granny. I'm coming back."

I clattered down the steps to the cabin and ran the gauntlet of tightly fitted beds, cupboard doors and the galley kitchen, pursued by the clicking of puppy claws on the metal floor. I launched myself through the rear door into my grandmother's waiting embrace. I may have cried a little, or maybe a lot. I said nothing, taking sanctuary in the deep hug.

With a reach back, the engine was cut off—we drifted in slow silence. Granny looked at the torn, bleeding ear and quizzical eyes watching us from the cabin and asked me, "who's your new friend?"

"I don't know Granny, but I think she saved you by biting the canal monster's tail right when it darted toward you."

The puppy took that as an opportunity to leap out and take a few frolicking jumps around us, spinning and glinting, her damp fur catching the sunlight. "She's like a little disco ball," laughed my grandmother.

She released me from her hug, patted her shirt pockets and produced another dip dab packet. "It's best if you don't tell your father," she said, "... about any of this."

And that's how Disco the whippet came to be part of the Redferne family. If I ask my grandmother now—when Disco and I visit her on one of her 'foggy days'—about the canal monster, she chuckles and says something like, "that's a funny story, child." It seems like I must have invented it, but then I look at the long-healed nick in Disco's ear and think maybe there is some truth to the story, to our secret day on the canal.

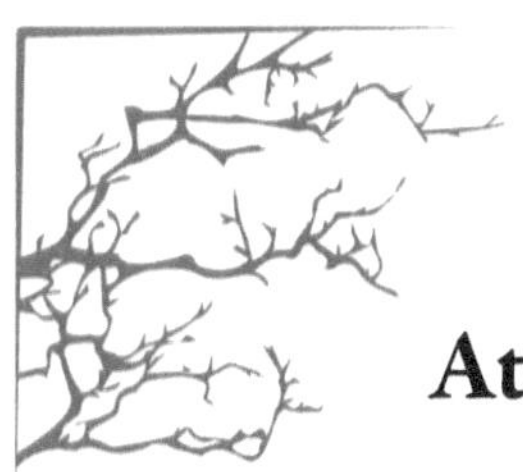

At Ashton Pond

Summer break sounds like fun, but it's just plain boring when your best friend goes away to stay at his grandmother's house, and you have no choice but to hang around with a goat all day. I wasn't exactly wishing myself back to school, but the action-packed days I had been dreaming about since March had failed to arrive.

"Templeton Redferne, you are a navigational hazard!"

I knew when my mother used my full name I was on the verge of receiving some major chastisement. And yes, I was a bit of a hazard, my back pressed on the kitchen floor, investigating the bottom of the sink. I was trying to figure out how the water drains away when you pull the rubber plug. But that tone of voice! My twelve-year-old frame exploded from prone to an escape point near the kitchen's back door.

"If you want to be bored, go be bored somewhere I'm not trying to clean," she added.

I peered across the kitchen island, where she stood with one hand in a yellow rubber glove. An eruption of red curls refused subjugation by the scarf tied severely just above her eyebrows. I wondered where the other glove had disappeared to. She probably did too. Uh oh, didn't I use a rubber glove as part of my vinegar and baking soda experiment?

One-gloved or two, I hesitated to push my luck and suggest something I'd like to do today. Safer to just keep quiet and find another venue for my scientific investigations. But there's nothing wrong with asking, is there? She taught me that herself!

"I could go to the movies."

She leaned her hip against the porcelain sink's edge and looked me up and down. "What's showing?"

Armed with an answer, I replied. But armed more in the sense of a butter knife, not a samurai sword. Before being forced off to his grandmother's house in Manchester, Eric told me his older sister had been talking up a movie she had seen. "I could see *The Exorcist*. It's on at the Middle Ides Cinema."

"*The Exorcist?*" My mother laughed. "They wouldn't let you in. You're too young. You don't even look twelve, because you're so cute, my darling. Plus, I heard it's really scary."

"But I *like* scary, mum. You know that."

She pondered. "Well, when I was a little girl, my friends and I used to go up to Ashton Pond, just beyond the ridge at the hilltop. It's spooky up there. You should take Vilhelm and go."

I tried a few excuses, but she had already decided. Her rubber glove abandoned, she packed a lunch, her many bangles and bracelets making familiar music as she plucked items from the refrigerator.

She handed me a small linen pouch, held closed with a clothes peg. "Just go up the hill. When you get to that tree there—with the reddish leaves and the wide-flung branches—turn left down the track and you'll get to the pond soon enough. You can't miss it.

"There's an army of frogs and toads up there—check them out. But don't drink the water or go in swimming. And especially don't try to catch any toads—look but *don't touch*. And no fishing!"

Vilhelm must have known something interesting was occurring, because there was a clopping sound from the yard and his narrow, bearded face appeared in the back door's window. He tracked me with his beady eyes as I grabbed a woven mat and three comic books that I rolled up and stuffed in my pocket.

Don't ask me why we didn't have a cat or a dog—or even a guinea pig—and instead were lumbered with a pet goat. I had asked myself and anyone else who would listen that same question many times already, without getting even a semi-satisfactory answer. But I guess Vilhelm was okay. His quirks ranged from falling down the back steps after drinking a half-bottle of unwatched brandy to sneaking into bed with me for a snuggle on cold winter nights. He had one black horn and one grey, his slender tangled white beard looking like a transplant from some Kung Fu master. And naturally he ate pretty much anything, including the neighbour's prized rosebushes—thorns and all—when he last escaped. He was decidedly goatish.

I left the house through the back door, calling, "Thanks, mum," without even a backward glance. Vilhelm and I set off on our adventure, speeding across the grassy yard and out the back gate through the warm summer air. I gripped the frayed rope that ultimately encircled Vilhelm and a rusty bell at his neck clanked begrudgingly as he half walked, half hopped his way across the small field to the foot of the hill that rose behind the house. I had to give little tugs on the rope every eight or ten steps to jostle him away from investigating weeds, insects, or his own hoof. Our shadows climbed ahead of us up the hillside. The rolled up mat and comic books in my pocket made my shadow look like a samurai, with sword strapped to my back and a dagger at my hip. Vilhelm's shadow looked like, well, a goat. Just a taller, skinnier goat, with a longer beard.

We paused for a breather about halfway up. My mother called it a hill, but I was having my own visions of needing a Sherpa and climbing axe if there was to be any hope of reaching the summit. The Ides Giant that we were skirting alongside was massive—the club-wielding giant's outline cut into the limestone of the hill contrasted against the yellowy-green of the long grasses we marched through—and we had only made it to his waist! I leaned over to catch my breath. Vilhelm discovered a blackened banana peel and two apple cores that an earlier adventurer had left behind. Probably their last meal before they got lost, never to be heard from again, I reckoned.

Soon enough we reached the scarlet-leafed tree. Its trunk was thick and gnarled, as if railroaded out of the town below for some misdemeanor and watched from here, wallowing in curmudgeonliness. We veered left along the track that headed along the hill's brow, me in one tire rut and Vilhelm in the other. Birds twittered and rustled. Midges and butterflies drifted in lazy navigation around us.

The trees lining the track's periphery closed ranks and towered over us. Only occasional sunlight shafts penetrated the canopy. I spotted the pond as we rounded a gentle bend in the track, but we needed to edge up to it to discern every detail. The sun had gone behind a cloud and there were wisps of mist in the air, making me squint as if peering through a gauze shroud.

Vilhelm ambled along, in knock-kneed bliss, but I noticed the background grew quieter and noisier at the same time. No birdsong reached my ears, but a chorus of frog and toad voices got louder with each step closer to the pond. We arrived. It wasn't *that* spooky, no match for a scary movie! It was ordinary, rippling darkly under the overcast sky, flanked by reeds at its marshy edges.

But the croaking grew louder still, which was odd. Normally, if I rustled in the reeds like this, any frogs nearby would stop their croaking and wheezing, only returning to full volume if I paused and posed motionless. And they tended to remain silent in the daytime, preferring to save their romance for the moon.

But mum was right, frogs and toads formed a patchwork skirt around the pond with surprising density. I spotted them with ease, their unrelenting calls drawing my attention. I let Vilhelm's rope dangle and introduced my shoes to the pond water as I wandered around its fringes, checking out the leaping, croaking, and splashing as I went. Frogs and toads of all complexions, sizes and voices frolicked.

Clouds still lurked overhead and curls of mist drifted directionless as I rolled out the mat which Vilhelm occupied with neither shame nor hesitation, leaving me to stake out one measly corner as my territory. I pocketed the clothes peg and started on my lunch. I laughed when I saw the trinket that mum had slipped into the lunch bag. It was a little toad carved out of dark stone with two fake rubies as eyes. She always did secret things like this for me—at school I would pocket little tokens like this before anyone could take notice, my hand returning to them throughout the day, warming at the thought of her.

I was indiscriminate in what or how I ate, so I foraged my way through the bread, cheese, and fruit like a marauding army before settling in for intense comic reading. My imagination fled into the realm of superheroes while Vilhelm munched on the delicacy otherwise known as the woven mat's fringe. I tuned out the croaking noises as I put in some imaginary crime-fighting work, contributing to Batman's eventual success.

After a while, I reclined on the mat, my head resting on the wiry hair of Vilhelm's flank, considering what to do next. The list of prohibited activities my mother had reeled off seemed over-long. Surely, it would be okay to catch just one or two of the toads, if I let them go and didn't try to smuggle them into my bedroom.

Everything I needed was at hand. After a two-footed encouragement to get Vilhelm off the mat, I rolled it up into a makeshift rod and attached the linen lunch bag to its end using the clothes peg. A sure-fire toad-catching device if I'd ever seen one! I pocketed the toad token, absently caressing its smooth, cool stone contours as I approached the first likely-looking clutch of amphibious prey.

They leapt from reed to reed and from one marshy tuft of grass to another as I extended my catcher and tried to snag one. At first, I found my prey too agile for my clumsy swiping technique. I spied a trio of toads sitting on a patch of floating vegetation, so I edged even closer, wading out until the cool pond water crept over the top of my shorts. With a quick flick of my improvised toad catcher, I snared one. It wriggled in the linen bag.

And then the croaking was replaced by dead silence.

My captive still wriggled as if obligated, but nothing else moved. No butterflies fluttered. No birds chirped. The loudest sound was the thickening mist, and it made only an imagined noise of sinister friction.

Vilhelm emitted a querulous bleat from the shore behind me, a whispered accusation about what was happening. His bell clinked once, twice. Although I dared not move, I could tell he scanned the area in apprehension. I moved my eyes as far left and right as feasible without turning my head but saw nothing unexpected. Uncertain, and with accelerating trepidation, remaining motionless seemed the best plan. I tried to minimize my breathing.

Ripples formed a short way in front of me, and the tips of a few reeds emerged through the black pond's surface, the drips of water falling from them making magnified sounds in the silence. They rose taller and taller until I realized they were not reeds and I started to tremble. They were the gently curling lashes of a grotesque and gigantic eyeball, each as long as my forearm and as thick as my rolled-up mat. Droplets of pond water scattered in all directions as the obscene eyelid flicked open.

The eyeball almost matched my height, with the bottom half still submerged, like me. It stared at me and I remained powerless to do anything but stare right back. Despite the warm summery day, the pond water seemed to be dropping in temperature. A warmth in my pants didn't even register as my own pee until much later. The eye reoriented itself as the rest of the massive toad head emerged, revealing a second frightful eyeball as a pair of fetid nostrils rose, almost grazing my face. They were like two slime-encrusted caverns, inches away. And still I stood rooted, not daring to do anything.

With a movement so sudden I thought it would be the last thing I ever witnessed, a wave crested over me as the giant jaws opened and a rumbling, raspy croak—felt more than heard—blasted me. I stumbled backward and a second primal croak trembled my clothes and blew my damp hair away from my face. Then the creature disappeared, submerged. Frogs, birds and insects sprang to life and voice again as if urged on by an invisible conductor. Neither Vilhelm nor I noticed. We were already running as fast as our legs and hooves would carry us, along the lane, past the thick-trunked tree and half-running, half-stumbling down the hill and into the back yard of our house. The mat, comics, lunch bag, and even Vilhelm's trusty rope were all lost somewhere between the house and Ashton Pond. My hand bled where I had been gripping the little jeweled toad trinket with all my will.

I wrenched open the back door and stumbled to my knees in the kitchen, with my drenched feet still dangling into the yard. Vilhelm howled a series of distressed bleats above me, his front hooves perched on my back. I was crying, laughing in hysterical relief, and trying to get some oxygen back into my system as I tried to string some words together. My mother knelt close beside me.

"Mom. I saw... we went... you won't believe me... giant eye..."

She hugged me and smoothed my frantic hair back onto my scalp. "That's the Undertoad, Templeton. I told you it was scary."

More Redferne
Adventures

The Redfernes will return in the full-length novel *Sky Lanterns over Nether Ides*. Find more details at https://pattisontelford.com

Don't miss out!

Visit the website below and you can sign up to receive emails whenever Pattison Telford publishes a new book. There's no charge and no obligation.

https://books2read.com/r/B-A-QGQJ-XOTCB

BOOKS 2 READ

Connecting independent readers to independent writers.

About the Author

If you like quirky adventure stories, I am writing for you. Quick pacing, characters that are appealing to Young Adult or adult readers alike, maybe a little bit of magic, and a few chuckles are all part of the journey.

Currently, I am writing stories about the Redferne family. The Redferne siblings and their dog, Disco, are thrust into a bit more responsibility and experience many more odd events than they are really prepared for, but they band together and struggle through. Although their town, Middle Ides, is fictitious, it is a combination of a number of places I have lived and visited, and the setting breathes life into their various adventures (and misadventures).

I live in Toronto, Canada, with my wife, two teenage sons, and snaggle-toothed dog. Previously living in in Scotland, England, and Australia has armed me with a considerable range of slang words and insults. I grew up playing basketball and have spent far too much time sitting in front of computer screens in my job as a Microsoft IT Consultant.

Read more at https://pattisontelford.com.